nickelodeon™

W9-CAW-025

PAW Patrol

PUPS
on a ROLL

Stories, Activities, and PAWsome Adventures!

we make books come alive®
pi kids® **Phoenix International Publications, Inc.**
Chicago • London • New York • Hamburg • Mexico City • Sydney

Illustrated by Fabrizio Petrossi and Harry Moore

Customer Service: 1-877-277-9441 or customerservice@pikidsmedia.com

Published by Phoenix International Publications, Inc.
8501 West Higgins Road   59 Gloucester Place
Chicago, Illinois 60631   London W1U 8JJ

PI Kids and *we make books come alive* are trademarks of Phoenix International Publications, Inc., and are registered in the United States.

Look and Find is a trademark of Phoenix International Publications, Inc., and is registered in the United States and Canada.

www.pikidsmedia.com

ISBN: 978-1-5037-5458-4

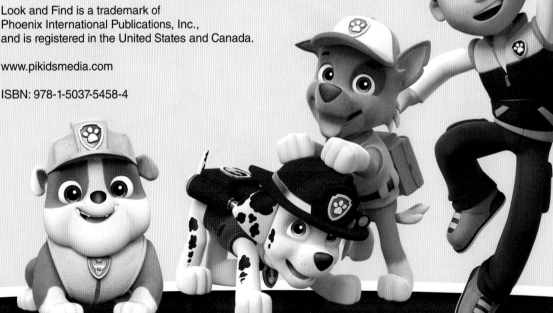

Table of Contents

Pups Save the Fireworks

Mayor Goodway and Chickaletta got a package in the mail. They were super excited—it was the fireworks for the Adventure Bay summer picnic! The box started to move and Mayor Goodway heard an "Oink!" That didn't seem right... suddenly six piglets jumped out of the box and quickly ran away!

Mayor Goodway knew just who to call—the PAW Patrol! Ryder called the pups to the Lookout and explained the situation. Then he came up with a plan!

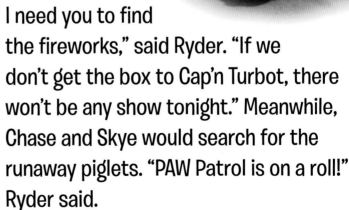

"Marshall, I need you to find the fireworks," said Ryder. "If we don't get the box to Cap'n Turbot, there won't be any show tonight." Meanwhile, Chase and Skye would search for the runaway piglets. "PAW Patrol is on a roll!" Ryder said.

Ryder and Marshall jumped in their vehicles and headed out to Farmer Yumi's farm to look for the fireworks. She had received a package of her own. It was her piglets. Or so she thought! When she opened the box, she found a delivery of apples! Ryder thought the apples were meant for Mr. Porter.

"Maybe he has the fireworks," said Marshall. Ryder and Marshall hurried to Mr. Porter's restaurant.

Meanwhile, Chase went to City Hall and spotted the piglets running around outside. He aimed his net launcher at one—but caught Mayor Goodway instead! Chase freed Mayor Goodway, and together they managed to catch one of the piglets.

Chase ran after another piglet, and he and the piglet *both* accidentally got caught in one of his nets! Well, at least two of the piglets were safe! Mayor Goodway fed the two pigs some corn to keep them happy.

Ryder and Marshall zoomed to town, only to find Mr. Porter opening what he thought was a box of apples. But it was a box of shampoo bottles for Katie at the Pet Parlor!

"She must have the fireworks," said Marshall. So he and Ryder hurried to the Pet Parlor.

At the beach, Skye was flying overhead in search of the missing piglets. She spotted two on the sand rolling in a blanket! She called Chase and he hurried to the beach. They'd caught four of the piglets—only two left!

At the Pet Parlor, Katie received a box...but it wasn't her shampoo. This box had a picture of fireworks on it. It had to be Mayor Goodway's missing package! Marshall took the box and brought it to Cap'n Turbot's boat.

Back at the beach, Chase found the fifth piglet—she was in the bay! Ryder turned his ATV into a jet ski to help lead the little piggy to safety. Now, where could the last piglet be?

Mayor Goodway said the last piglet must be tired and hungry by now. This gave Ryder an idea. He got Mayor Goodway to hold out a piece of corn and asked Chase to do an impression of a pig on his megaphone.

SNIFF!

OINK!

OINK!

OINK!

The piglet heard the call and smelled the corn. He ran up to Mayor Goodway and Chase. They'd found the last little piglet!

It was almost time for the fireworks show! Everyone headed to the beach to watch. Mayor Goodway thanked Ryder and the PAW Patrol for saving the summer picnic. From out in the bay on his boat, Cap'n Turbot set off the fireworks, and as they lit up the night sky, everyone cheered. What an awesome show!

Three barks for teamwork!

Oh no! Mayor Goodway can't find Chickaletta anywhere! Marshall climbs his ladder to search the trees. Can you find Chickaletta and these other birds, too?

this pigeon

blue jay

sparrow

rooster

cardinal

Chickaletta

Everyone is excited about the Adventure Bay bake sale!

Special!

Katie and Alex were playing with Rocky and Zuma at the beach when Alex hit his volleyball across the road. It landed on the sand—and some little green heads popped out. They were baby sea turtles hatching from their eggs! The sea turtles needed a safe way to cross the road and get to the sea.

Rocky and Zuma raced off to find Ryder. After hearing the news, Ryder called all the pups. "PAW Patrol, to the Lookout!" he said. Ryder needed Chase to direct the traffic so the turtles could safely cross the road.

"These paws uphold the laws," Chase said.

"Rubble, we need to build a way for the turtles to get to the water without crossing the road," Ryder said.

"Rubble on the double!" Rubble replied.

Meanwhile, more tiny sea turtles had hatched and were heading toward the sea! Chase stopped the traffic to let the turtles cross. Then Ryder spotted an opening leading to a tunnel under the road. It was blocked with sand. The babies couldn't get into the tunnel, and that's why they were crossing the road instead! He asked Rubble to dig it out.

"Once the tunnel reopens, the turtles never have to cross the road again," Chase said.

"Let's dig it," Rubble said. He extended the bucket arm scoop from his Pup Pack and got busy clearing the tunnel.

While everyone else was busy, Alex was bored. He spotted Zuma's windsurfer and took it into the sea, but a sudden gust of wind lifted him up into the sky! "Help!" he cried.

"This pup's gotta fly!" said Skye, opening the wings on her Pup Pack. She swooped toward Alex and guided him safely back to the beach.

"Well done, Skye!" everyone shouted.

Rubble finished digging the tunnel, and streams of baby sea turtles started coming through.

"I knew you could do it!" said Ryder. "I think you pups really deserve some beach time!"

With the turtles safe and sound, they all built a sandcastle. What an excellent day!

Just yelp for help!

Picture Puzzle

The pups spend a PAWsitively relaxing day at the beach!

Answer key: Rubble's inner tube, Marshall's sunglasses, Skye's sunglasses, green shell on the left, Rocky's Pup Pack, shell in front of Skye, Zuma's position, soccer ball, flag, crab

Ready, set, get wet! Zuma races to Cap'n Turbot's boat to patch a leak. Rocky stays behind—and he stays nice and dry! Find these other animals in the sand, sea, or sky:

dolphin

seagull

turtle

whale

pelican

crab

Pups Save the Space Alien

One night, Ryder, Rocky, and Skye were looking at the stars, when suddenly a ball of light fell through the sky! "That looks like some kind of spaceship," said Ryder.

The spaceship crash-landed on Farmer Yumi's cow shed, to the surprise of Bettina, the cow. The frightened alien inside the spaceship sucked poor Bettina into a big green bubble and left her floating in the sky!

Mayor Goodway was on her way home from Farmer Yumi's house when she saw Bettina hanging in the air! She quickly called Ryder and the PAW Patrol for help.

"We're on it, Mayor Goodway!" said Ryder. He called the sleeping PAW Patrol and they raced to the Lookout. Ryder told the pups about the strange spaceship that had landed at Farmer Yumi's.

For this mission, Ryder needed Chase's spy skills to find the pilot of the spaceship. "Super Spy Chase is on the case!" said Chase.

"And I'll need you to fix whatever it is that fell from the sky," Ryder said to fix-it pup Rocky. With that, Chase, Rocky, and Ryder all raced to Farmer Yumi's.

When Ryder and the pups arrived at Farmer Yumi's, they found Bettina in her bubble—and the broken spaceship. Chase used his zip line suction cups to burst the bubble and free Bettina. "Chase, now I need you to use your spy gear to find the pilot of that spaceship," said Ryder.

"Yes sir, Ryder sir!" replied Chase.

Chase followed some footprints and found Mayor Goodway and Chickaletta in Farmer Yumi's fields. They were stuck in a floating green bubble, too! "How did you get up there?" asked Chase.

"A little green space alien beamed us up," she said. Chase couldn't believe his ears. A real space alien! He quickly rescued Mayor Goodway from the green bubble, put on his night vision goggles, and went to look for the alien in Farmer Yumi's fields.

Moo!

Chase found the alien hiding in a field of watermelons. The alien was so scared, he sucked Chase into a floating green bubble and quickly ran away!

beep bop

beep bop

Meanwhile, at the barn, Rocky was using objects from his truck to finish fixing the spaceship.

"Looks like we're done here. I'll go and check on Chase," said Ryder.

Chase was still stuck in the green bubble. Suddenly, he remembered he could use the zip line to free himself, just like he had done for Bettina and Mayor Goodway. He shot the zip line out of his spy gear and landed safely back on the ground.

Woo-hoo!

We've got a visitor at the Lookout.

Beep, beep, beep!

Ryder soon found Chase, and the police pup told him all about the alien. Just then, Ryder got a call on his Pup Pad. It was Skye—the alien was at the Lookout! "We're on our way," said Ryder.

The alien thought that the Lookout was another spaceship and he was trying to fly it home!

"I'm sorry, but that won't work," Ryder told the lost alien.

Ryder called Rocky to see if the spaceship was ready. Suddenly Rocky appeared at the Lookout's window in the fixed spaceship! "Just yelp—or beep, beep, beep—for help!" said Ryder to the happy alien.

The alien took the PAW Patrol for a ride before leaving Adventure Bay and heading home.

wHOOSH!

Let's take to the sky!

Look and Find

Come fly with Skye, PAW Patrol's pilot! She is a daredevil cockapoo who swoops through the sky! Can you find her and these other aerial items?

plane

this butterfly

eagle

helicopter

hot-air balloon

kite

Look and Find

Skye flies over Adventure Bay to look for some farm friends who have roamed away from a sleepover. Can you help her find them?

goat

this sheep

this duck

this pig

this cow

this sheep

Pit Crew Pups

At Mr. Porter's restaurant, Alex was having fun making a trike from boxes and spare things he found lying around. He couldn't wait to show off his new super-trike to his grandpa. It had a vegetable box for a seat and pizza paddles for brakes! Alex was desperate to try out his new invention, but as soon as he tried to ride it, it broke into pieces.

Alex tried to run into the road to pick up the pieces, but Mr. Porter stopped him. It was too dangerous! Mr. Porter saw how upset Alex was about the broken trike, so he called Ryder and the PAW Patrol.

Ryder and the pups got to work on the broken trike. Chase blocked off the street, and Rocky picked up the broken pieces. Back at the Lookout, the PAW Patrol put the super-trike back together. Rocky replaced the paddles with real brakes, added a bell, and even got a brand new helmet for Alex to wear!

Soon the super-trike was ready. Ryder warned Alex to take it slow, but Alex pedaled away as fast as he could. His trike was heading straight toward a busy road! Suddenly, Alex was going down a hill and the trike was going fast. Really, really fast! Alex lost control of the trike. Chase quickly built a roadblock, and Skye swooped in to stop Alex. He was safe! The PAW Patrol had saved the day!

To celebrate, Ryder suggested they head over to the lemonade stand.

"Let's race on over," said Alex. But then he remembered: sometimes it is best to take it slow!

Let's roll!

All-Star Pups

The PAW Patrol were busy getting ready for a sports competition. They were playing soccer against Ringmaster Raimundo and his team of monkeys! The pups were very excited about the game.

Suddenly, Ryder got a call from Mayor Goodway. The sprinkler system had been left on all night and the sports field was covered in mud! "We won't be able to play on this field for days," cried Mayor Goodway.

"Don't worry, Mayor," said Ryder. "We'll find a new place to have the game."

Ryder called the pups to the PAW Patroller to hash out a plan. They came up with a great idea: Farmer Al's pasture! Ryder and the pups jumped into their vehicles and raced to Farmer Al's.

Rubble got busy clearing the pasture of rocks, while Marshall used his paint cannons to draw the lines for the soccer game. Soon the field was ready for the competition!

Suddenly an eagle swooped down and stole the ball from Marshall! Ryder, Skye, and Everest hopped in their vehicles and zoomed to the mountain to rescue it. In her copter, Skye lured the eagle away from its nest, while Everest scaled the mountain to grab the ball. That's when Everest saw that the eagle took the ball so her babies could have a toy! The trio had an awesome idea. Skye gave the baby eagles her favorite toy mouse, so the babies had something to play with and the PAW Patrol could have their ball.

Back in the pasture, the PAW Patrol and the monkeys finished their game. Marshall scored two goals! The PAW Patrol saved the day AND won the game!

Pups away!

Buckle up! It's time for an Adventure Bay road race. When Alex needs help getting his trike back on the road, Chase is on the case! Find these vehicles behind Chase's roadblock:

Rocky's recycling truck

Skye's helicopter

Marshall's fire truck

Zuma's hovercraft

Rubble's digger

Everest's snowplow

Who wants to play? The pups love to hit the Pup Park with Ryder. Run, ride, skate, and slide along with the PAW Patrol as you find these playground things:

jump rope

slide

tetherball

skateboard

ball

wagon

Pups Save the Fall Festival

It was almost time for the Fall Festival in Adventure Bay! Chase and Marshall were helping Farmer Yumi collect her apples and pumpkins, but some of the branches were too high for the pups to reach the apples.

Then Marshall got an idea. He jumped onto a bale of hay and grabbed onto a high branch with his teeth. But the branch was too springy, and it popped Marshall into the air! He flew over the orchard and landed in the pumpkin patch.

Mooo!

Bettina the cow started mooing sadly. "All that switching and twitching means that bad weather is coming, and that won't be good for the apples," said Farmer Yumi. She checked the forecast on her phone—snow was on the way!

They needed to get all the apples and pumpkins inside before the snow came. Otherwise the fruit would freeze and be ruined, and they wouldn't have apples or pumpkins for the festival.

"It'll take the three of us too long," said Farmer Yumi.

"Ryder and the PAW Patrol can help!" said Chase.

Upon hearing about the snowstorm, Ryder called all the pups to the Lookout.

"Marshall, we need you and your ladder to reach the fruit in the high branches," Ryder said. Then he asked Rubble to carry the fruit to the barn in his digger. He needed help from the rest of PAW Patrol, too! "This is a job big enough for every pup," he said. They all jumped in their vehicles and headed to Farmer Yumi's farm.

Rocky went to look for something to get the apples to the barn quicker.

"What can I do?" asked Chase.

"Just see what needs doing and pitch in," said Ryder.

Chase tried to collect apple baskets, but Rubble could push all the baskets at once with his digger. Next, Chase tried to help collect pumpkins, but Skye and Zuma were already rolling them down the hill, and he almost got hit!

WHOA!

"There must be something I can do," said Chase. Suddenly, Marshall ran by with an apple basket stuck on his head. He fell right into the path of the rolling pumpkins, and they sent him flying!

Just then, Rubble arrived with lots of apples in his digger and saw Marshall speeding toward him! He hit the brakes, but that sent the apples flying out of the digger. Skye, Zuma, and Chase all ducked down, but poor Marshall fell into another pile of pumpkins!

"Oh no!" said Rocky. "The farm is a mess." The pups agreed that this wasn't how to get the job done. They needed some organization.

"Chase, now I've got a job for you," said Ryder. He asked the police pup to direct traffic, to make sure nothing like this happened again.

Chase used his megaphone to let everyone know when to do their job. Meanwhile, Rocky used a drainpipe he'd found to help the pups get apples into the baskets really quickly! The PAW Patrol collected the apples in no time, but there were still a lot of pumpkins to collect.

Suddenly, it started to turn cold—the pups were running out of time! "Pumpkin rolling contest!" yelled Chase. The PAW Patrol hurried to the pumpkin patch, but Marshall lost control and ended up with another pumpkin on his head!

Just as the snow started to fall, the PAW Patrol finished the job. All the apples and pumpkins were in the barn.

"Ryder, you and the pups saved the day!" said Farmer Yumi.

The next day at the festival, everyone had fun bobbing for apples and eating pumpkin pie! The Fall Festival was saved, thanks to the PAW Patrol!

The PAW Patrol is on the

Farmer Yumi needs a helping hand—or paw—at harvest time. Rubble digs in with his bulldozer. Help find signs for these farm-fresh foods:

apples

blueberries

strawberries

pears

pumpkins

cherries

Look and Find®

The PAW Patrol has fixed the barn—just in time for Farmer Al and Farmer Yumi's wedding! Can you find these wonderful wedding things?

this bouquet

this gift

cake

disco ball

this corn decoration

this gift

When anyone needs help, the pups are there to lend a paw!

Can you help find 10 differences between the pictures?

Pups Save Skye

One morning, Skye set out to Jake's Mountain to see her friend Ace. Ace was a stunt pilot and had some new tricks to show off. But it was very stormy, and Skye was soon in trouble! The wind blew her into a tree, knocking off her Pup Tag. Skye looked back to see where it had landed, but then she crashed into the ground, squashing one of her wings!

"That wing is too bent to fly," said Skye sadly. Her paw was hurting, too, and without her Pup Tag, she couldn't call Ryder. It looked like she would have to hike all the way to Jake's chalet.

Up at the top of the mountain, Everest was worried. "I'm afraid something has happened to Skye in the storm," she told Ace. Ace decided to call Ryder.

Ryder listened while Ace explained.

"Skye didn't answer when I called her!" Everest told him.

"Don't worry," Ryder said. "We'll find her." He quickly called the other pups to the Lookout!

Once the pups were ready for action, Ryder told them that Skye was missing. He needed Everest to head down the mountain and search for the lost pup.

"Ace, can you help, too?" asked Ryder.

"You've got it, Ryder!" said Ace.

Ryder also needed Chase's help to sniff out Skye's trail.

"Chase is on the case!" said Chase. The PAW Patrol and Ace set off, determined to find their friend!

Skye was getting very cold and tired as she hiked. She found a tree to rest under for a moment, and three little bunnies came to keep her company!

As Ace was flying through the mountains, she noticed a crash site near Bear Rock.

"I know the spot," said Ryder. Skye must be nearby!

The way to Bear Rock was too steep for Ryder and Chase to climb, so Chase sent his drone. The drone found Skye's paw prints, but still no sign of the pup!

Luckily, Skye heard the drone. "Here I am!" she called, waving.

Everest followed the sound of the drone and soon spotted Skye. "I can see her," she told Ryder through her Pup Tag. "Hang on, Skye!"

Everest sent down her sled and Skye jumped on. "You'll be cozy and warm in no time," said Everest, pulling the sled back up the mountain. Skye had been rescued!

ZoooM!

"Hot cocoa and milk for my coolest pals," said Jake when they were all safely in his chalet. Ryder found Skye's Pup Tag and fastened it back around her neck.

"Now that everyone is here and the storm is over, who wants to watch a little trick-flying?" asked Ace.

Everyone cheered and went outside to watch. Ace did some amazing tricks, looping across the sky in her plane. It was a pup-tastic end to a very busy day!

NeoOWW!

To the Lookout!

Look and Find

Ice or snow, Everest is ready to go! Everest is playing a game of hide-and-seek with the other rescue pups. Can you find these friends?

Tracker

Marshall

Rubble

Rocky

Skye

Chase

Uh-oh! Two polar bear babies have drifted away on the ice. Help Skye and Everest find them and these other friends:

mama bear

Ryder

Jake

this baby bear

this baby bear

Cap'n Turbot

Picture Puzzle

After a busy day, the pups gather around the campfire.

Find 10 things that are different in these cozy scenes.

It was time for the annual Mayor's Hot-Air Balloon Race, and Mayor Goodway had entered the contest. Even though she was afraid of heights, she was hoping to beat her great rival from Foggy Bottom, Mayor Humdinger. However, her hot-air balloon had a giant hole!

Luckily, the PAW Patrol was there to help. Rocky reused a piece of Zuma's old surf kite to patch up the hole, so the hot-air balloon was ready to fly.

The balloon started rising up in the air, but Mayor Goodway was scared and couldn't control it. Ryder called Skye to get him to the mayor. They would do the race together! With Ryder connected by a harness and cable, Skye flew up to the hot-air balloon and swung him safely into the basket.

The race had already started, and their hot-air balloon was far behind Mayor Humdinger's! When Ryder asked if she still wanted to be in the race, Mayor Goodway shouted, "In it to win it!" There was no stopping the dynamic duo from Adventure Bay!

Ryder let the hot-air balloon rise high up into the air where the winds were stronger...and Mayor Goodway didn't let her fear of heights stop them. They started to catch up with Mayor Humdinger! They went up and over Jake's Mountain, moving fast. They were getting closer and closer to Mayor Humdinger, and suddenly they passed him—just in time to cross the finish line!

Mayor Goodway won the blue ribbon, but she happily handed it straight to Ryder and the PAW Patrol—a reward for saving the day!

PAW Patrol, ready for

Pups Turn on the Lights

One windy day, Ryder and the pups were at Katie's Pet Parlor. They were super excited because it was Chase's birthday and they were throwing him a surprise party. Rocky was putting up decorations, Katie was making the cake, and Marshall was keeping Chase busy so he wouldn't find out the plan.

All of a sudden, they were plunged into darkness. There was a power outage in Adventure Bay! Without electricity, they couldn't make the cake or play music. Chase's party would be ruined!

Ryder called the pups to the Lookout, but without electricity, the elevator wasn't working. Using Marshall's ladder, Ryder climbed into the Lookout. He looked through the periscope and saw that the wind turbine had a broken blade. Ryder decided Rocky and Marshall would fix the blade...then he secretly let Skye, Zuma, and Rubble know they should continue getting ready for the party.

The street traffic was chaos! Without traffic lights to guide them, no one knew when to drive, wait, or walk. Luckily, Chase the police pup was there to direct traffic!

Meanwhile, at the Pet Parlor, the pups were setting up the party. They even invented lots of games to play in the dark!

On the other side of town, Ryder, Rocky, and Marshall repaired the wind turbine using Zuma's old surfboard as a blade. Don't lose it, reuse it!

With the surfboard in place, the turbine started to move, power was restored, and the lights came back on. Hooray! Chase started to get ready to leave when Ryder called and asked him to come to the Pet Parlor right away! Chase zoomed through town. He rushed through the Pet Parlor doors and...

"Happy Birthday!" the pups shouted. Chase couldn't believe it! There hadn't been time to bake a cake, so Katie brought out a cake made of pup treats and the pups dug in. Skye turned off the lights so that they could play some new games in the dark. Maybe power outages weren't so bad, after all!

Call the
PAW
Patrol!

When the Kitty Catastrophe Crew swipes the carnival prizes, Skye takes to the sky to find them! Can you find these colorful bunny toys?

pink toy

purple toy

green toy

orange toy

yellow toy

blue toy

Picture Puzzle

These pals know how to party!

Answer key: green streamer, sun, cloud, bunny, gift with blue bow, Marshall's hat, candles, bow on food dish, gift with yellow bow, Tracker's hat

Pups Save a Parrot

The PAW Patrol was on the way to help their friend Carlos in the jungle. His parrot had disappeared! When they arrived, Ryder spotted a harpy eagle in a tree.

The PAW Patroller reached the spot where Carlos and Mandy the monkey were waiting.

"Has your parrot come back yet?" asked Ryder.

"No, I haven't seen Mateo at all," Carlos replied sadly. He was worried about Mateo being alone in the jungle, especially because of the harpy eagle. Little Mateo was no match for a bird that big!

Ryder gathered the pups in the PAW Patroller. They were going to save Mateo! "Look for his blue and red colors," said Ryder. Carlos also told them that he had trained Mateo to SQUAWK for help!

"Skye, I need you and your helicopter to look for Mateo from the air," said Ryder. Then he told Chase to use his spy drone to search the treetops, and Marshall to use his ladder to look among the leaves.

Marshall was racing through the jungle when he spotted something red, high up in the tree. When he got up closer he realized that it wasn't a parrot, but a big red plant.

Uh-oh! Marshall slipped and slid down his ladder! His red helmet came off, and mischievous Mandy the monkey grabbed it and ran off into the jungle!

Chase used his spy drone to search the treetops for Mateo. He found something red, but after a closer look, he saw that it was just Mandy wearing Marshall's hard hat!

Meanwhile, Skye was searching the skies in her helicopter. The harpy eagle spotted her and started chasing her! Skye dove in and out of the trees and finally managed to escape to the other side of the jungle.

Skye radioed in to Ryder. "I think I found him," she said. Mateo was flying toward the jungle ruins.

"On our way, Skye!" said Ryder. The PAW Patrol arrived at the ruins with Carlos and Mandy.

"That's Marshall's hat," Carlos said, plucking the red helmet off the monkey's head and handing it to the rightful owner.

Mateo landed on the edge of one of the ruins. Marshall climbed up to rescue him. When he got to the top, Marshall let out a gasp. "An egg!"

Carlos's parrot was a she, and she was having a baby! They decided to call her Matea from then on!

Carlos and the PAW Patrol spent the night at the ruins to protect Matea's egg from the scary eagle. In the morning, the egg had hatched, and Matea had a very cute baby parrot!

Suddenly, the PAW Patrol heard a loud screech. It was the harpy eagle flying overhead! Matea's baby parrot was very scared and ran away, straight toward the edge of the ruins.

"Watch out!" Carlos shouted.

Ryder and the PAW Patrol sprang into action. "We'll deal with the eagle. Carlos, you make sure the baby bird doesn't fall," said Ryder.

The eagle took a dive at the baby bird, so Chase bark, bark, barked and scared it away!

Next, Chase used his drone to distract the harpy eagle.

"Nice flying, Chase! That will keep the eagle too far away to do any damage to the parrots," said Ryder.

Suddenly, the baby parrot tumbled over the side of the ruins! Luckily, Carlos was at the bottom to catch him.

"I've got you!" Carlos said. Matea and the baby bird were back together. "Thanks to you pups, Matea and the chick are both safe and sound!" said Carlos.

PAW Patrol— let's roll!

Ahoy! The pups are on a pirate adventure!

Take out your spyglass and spot 10 differences between the pirate pictures.

PAW Patrol is on a roll, heading out on a new mission!

Your mission: spot 10 differences between the pictures!

Answer key: *fire truck, Rocky's truck, Chase, cones, Zuma's hovercraft, hovercraft arm, cloud, Skye, tree, flower*

Pups Save Friendship Day

It was Friendship Day! The pups were busy making friendship cards for everyone in town.

"Great job, pups!" said Ryder.

Rubble and Marshall headed to the post office to mail the cards.

"It will be my delight to deliver them!" said Mr. Postman.

"These cards just go to show that Adventure Bay is the friendliest town around!" added Mayor Goodway proudly.

"Ha! No place is as friendly as Foggy Bottom!" said Mayor Humdinger. One of the mayor's mean cats launched some mail at Mr. Postman, knocking him over so he twisted his ankle! OUCH! How were all the cards going to get delivered?

Mayor Humdinger challenged Mayor Goodway to a friend-off! Whichever town came up with the ultimate Friendship Day gift would win the title of the friendliest town.

Mayor Goodway needed help. All the friendship cards needed to be delivered, AND she needed an ultimate friendship gift, too. She knew just who to call: Ryder!

"We're going to need all paws on deck!" Ryder told the pups. They were going to deliver the mail!

As the pups loaded up the cards, Mayor Goodway appeared carrying an enormous cake made from every single cake at Mr. Porter's shop. "I smooshed them all together," she explained. It was the ultimate friendship gift. The cake had to get to Foggy Bottom, and fast!

Meanwhile, Mayor Humdinger decided to send Adventure Bay some friendship baskets. He filled them with candy and attached balloons. While his back was turned, some bunnies hopped in to nibble at the candy and accidentally untied the strings holding down the baskets. The baskets started to float away—all the way to Adventure Bay. Skye had to save the bunnies!

Chase launched his net between two trees. BOING! Skye used her helicopter blades to blow the baskets toward Chase. Then he used his ball cannon to burst the balloons and catch the bunnies in the net!

Chase still had the giant cake to deliver. He drove toward Foggy Bottom, but Mayor Humdinger had left nails on the road. POP! Chase's tires were punctured, and the cake flew forward! SPLAT!

"This is a cake-tastrophe!" Chase said.

Ryder, Rocky, and Mayor Goodway raced to the scene. "The cake is ruined!" said the mayor.

They couldn't let mean Mayor Humdinger win! Luckily, Rocky had a spatula. He used his skills to reshape the cake into... Mayor Humdinger!

Mayor Humdinger's eyes filled with tears. "That's the most beautiful thing I've ever seen," he said. But he still thought Foggy Bottom's gift was better! It was a giant balloon bouquet. Then the wind blew and lifted him and the balloons right up in the air. Mayor Goodway tried to pull him down, but she was lifted into the air, too!

Skye used her helicopter blades to blow the mayors back toward Ryder, Chase, and Rocky. Chase used his ball cannon once again to burst some of the balloons. POP! POP! POP! The mayors floated safely back to earth!

"You tried to save me!" said Mayor Humdinger. "That's the nicest thing anyone has ever done for me."

Mayor Goodway smiled at him. "That's what friends do for each other."

"You mean you and I are friends?" asked Mayor Humdinger.

"Of course!" said Mayor Goodway. "But if you were a bit nicer, nice things might happen a bit more!"

Everyone learned that the ultimate Friendship Day gift was...friendship!

PAW Patrol
to the

PAW Patrol is on a roll! Ryder and the pups are heading out of the Lookout to help around Adventure Bay. Can you find each pup?

Zuma

Skye

Rubble

Everest

Chase

Marshall

Rocky

It's time to gather the pups
at the Lookout!

Whenever there's trouble in Adventure Ba...
Ryder and PAW Patrol will set things righ...

Ready for another ruff-ruff rescue?

Go back to the beginning to read the book again!